Noah's Shark

WITHDRAWN

Noah's Shark

by Alan Durant
and Holly Surplice

First published 2009
Evans Brothers Limited
2A Portman Mansions
Chiltern St
London W1U 6NR

Durant, Alan, 1958-
  Noah's shark. -- (Skylarks)
  1. Children's stories.
  I. Title II. Series
  823.9'14-dc22

ISBN-13: 978 0 23 7 53904 7 (HB)
ISBN-13: 978 0 23 7 53891 0 (PB)

Printed in China by New Era Printing Co. Ltd

Series Editor: Louise John
Design: Robert Walster
Production: Jenny Mulvanny

Contents

Chapter One

Once, way back, there was this guy called Noah and he was fed up. He was fed up with the people who lived in his world, because they were making a right mess of things. They were dumping filth in the rivers, ripping up all the forests and killing off animals like there was no tomorrow.

One day, this guy Noah had had enough. He was at the end of his tether.

"That's it," he said. "I'm not staying here any longer. I'm going to build myself a boat and go and find another place to live."

So he did.

He started building his boat that very day. There was plenty of wood, too, with all the trees that had been cut down.

Noah built and he built. Night and day, he built, burning the candle at both ends. He was determined to finish that boat as soon as possible. His family helped him, but no one else. Well, everyone else thought he was nuts, crazy, cuckoo!

"What are you doing, Noah?" they asked.

"I'm building a boat," said Noah.

"A boat?" they scoffed. "What do you want a boat for?"

"So I can go over the sea," said Noah.

"Go over the sea!" they laughed. "What d'you think you are? A fish?"

"Hey, hear this, guys!" they cried.

"Noah thinks he's a fish!"

Well, everyone thought this was a really cool joke. Every time they passed Noah's place they made fishy faces and swishy noises and made out like they could smell something kind of funny.

"Is that fish we smell?" they'd say. Then they'd roar with laughter.

But old Noah, he just ignored them and got on with his building.

Chapter Two

The days passed into weeks, the weeks into months until, finally, Noah's boat was finished. It was huge, bigger than a house, bigger than a school. Now, why did he need a boat that big, you might wonder? Did he have an enormous family? Well, no, he didn't.

The reason he made his boat so big was that he wanted to invite some of his animal friends to sail with him. So, when he'd packed his boat with food and drink and clothes and all the things he'd need on his long voyage, he put up a notice:

Noah's boat will be sailing tomorrow morning at dawn. Any animals wishing to join him should show up an hour before sunrise. COUPLES ONLY! Latecomers will not be admitted.

Next morning, an hour before sunrise, there was a long, long queue leading to Noah's boat. All kinds of animals had come along. They couldn't wait to get away. They knew that if they stayed, then pretty soon they'd be dead meat.

Noah was delighted to see so many animals. He got them to board the boat in their pairs, two by two, while he wrote down their names on his passenger list.

"Welcome aboard!" he'd say, and on
they'd go.

Mr and Mrs Giraffe, he wrote, Mr and
Mrs Armadillo, Mr and Mrs Dodo, Mr
and Mrs Rabbit, Mr and Mrs Donkey,
Mr and Mrs Caterpillar, Mr and Mrs
Wombat, Mr and Mrs Zebra, and so on.

Pair after pair, they boarded Noah's boat, until there was only one animal left.

"Mrs Shark," said the creature.

"Mrs Shark?" said Noah. He peered at the creature. Then he peered at the empty space beside it. "Where's Mr Shark?" he asked.

"Ah," said the shark. "Um, well, in here." She opened her mouth wide, showing lots of very sharp teeth.

"In there?" said Noah.

"Yes," said the shark, looking sheepish. "I, er, swallowed him."

"You swallowed him!" cried Noah.

"It was an accident," said the shark. "He just sort of slipped in."

Noah shook his head. "I'm sorry," he said. "It's couples only. I can't let you on."

"Oh, please," begged the shark. "Please take me with you. I can't stay here. There's nothing to eat. I'll starve."

"I'm sorry," Noah said again. "You can't come on."

A large tear splashed from the shark's eye. "I beg you," she said. "I'll work

17

for my passage. I'll do anything you say. Please."

Now Noah was a real softy at heart and he couldn't bear to see a creature in distress.

"Oh, alright," he said. "You can come with us. But you'll have to work hard."

"I will, I will!" cried the shark, and on she slithered.

Now Noah's boat was full. He pulled up the gangplank and prepared to leave, waving goodbye to his old world. A few people had turned up to watch him go.

"'Bye, Noah, you old fish!" they shouted. Then they sniggered. They didn't reckon he'd get very far. He'd end up at the bottom of the sea,

they reckoned – and good riddance.
Now moany old Noah was gone, they
could have some fun. They could really
let their hair down.

But, as it happened, things didn't turn out so well. The next day there was a massive downpour of acid rain and the world was completely flooded with poisoned water and everyone drowned. Only Noah and his passengers survived, sailing on the sea, as the rain came down and down.

Chapter Three

For the first few weeks of the voyage
everything went well on Noah's boat.
The animals were happy that they had
escaped and everyone was looking
forward to their new life in a new world.
Noah was pleased as Punch to be
captain of such a happy boat.

Noah's shark, meanwhile, worked very hard. She was especially good at chewing through knots and she didn't get seasick like the rest of the crew. Life on the sea suited her, she quickly decided. There was just one thing she didn't care for and that was the food. Noah had stocked up with lots of fruit and vegetables and biscuits, but no meat. He'd brought no meat at all. Animals were his friends, he said, and he couldn't eat his friends. Now, this was all very well, thought the shark, but what if you didn't really like fruit or vegetables or biscuits? What then?

As the days went by, Noah's shark grew more and more hungry. She needed something proper to eat. After all, she thought, she was a worker,

she had to keep her strength up. But
what could she do?

One night, Noah sent his shark down
to the passenger lounge to check that
everyone was OK. She slithered along
the rows of sleeping animals and her
mouth started to water. She suddenly

started to imagine that she was in a giant fridge, surrounded by juicy joints of meat... At last, she could bear it no more. Just before the door, she stopped, opened her mouth and swallowed a dodo.

Next morning, Noah took the register as usual. When he shouted for Mr Dodo, there was no reply.

"Are you there, Mr Dodo?" he said.
"Where is Mr Dodo?"

"He's gone," said Mrs Dodo. "I woke
up this morning and he'd simply
disappeared." She sniffed sadly.

"Oh dear," said Noah. "Oh dear, oh
dear." He put his arm round Mrs Dodo.
Then he turned to face all the other
animals. "Does anyone know what's
happened to Mr Dodo?" he asked.

Everyone looked at each other and shook their heads. Everyone, except Noah's shark. She looked down at the floor and blushed. Noah gazed at her.

"Mrs Shark," said Noah, "do you know what happened to Mr Dodo?"

Noah's shark nodded. "I swallowed him," she said. "It was an accident. I opened my mouth and he just sort of slipped in."

"Just like Mr Shark," said Noah.

"Exactly," said Noah's shark.

"Hmm," said Noah sternly, "this is not good."

"It won't happen again," said Noah's shark. "I promise."

"It better not," said Noah, "or you'll be off this boat as quick as a flash."

The next morning, however, Mrs Dodo was gone.

"Mrs Shark, did you swallow Mrs Dodo?" Noah demanded.

"Well, yes," said Noah's shark. "I did. But I thought it was for the best."

"For the best?" said Noah. He couldn't believe his ears.

"Well, one dodo was no good without the other, was it?" said Noah's shark. "They weren't a couple any more. At least they're together now." She looked down at her full stomach.

Noah shook his head. "When I used to be a teacher," he said, "a boy once told me that his hamster had eaten his homework. That was a terrible excuse, but yours is worse. In my new world, dodos will be extinct. There will be no dodos and it is all your fault."

"I'm sorry," said Noah's shark,

looking sheepish. "It won't happen again. I promise."

"It better not," said Noah, "or you'll be off this boat. I mean it this time."

Chapter Four

For a few days, life on Noah's boat returned to normal. No animals disappeared and no names were struck off the register. Noah's shark worked harder than ever to try to make up for swallowing the dodos. But the harder she worked, the bigger her appetite got.

Soon she was starving again.

The next animals to vanish were Mr and Mrs Rabbit.

"You ate them both?" cried Noah.

"Well, one was no good without the other," explained Noah's shark.

"Not that excuse again," said Noah. "Now rabbits will also be extinct in my new world." He was about to add that this time the shark really would have to go, when a small, fierce voice stopped him in his tracks.

"Excuse me," it said. "Did you say rabbits stink? Because we don't you know. We're very clean."

For a moment Noah stared at the little creature as if he were looking at a ghost. Then he realised: Mr and Mrs Rabbit had bred and he was looking at

their babies. Thank goodness rabbits
bred so fast, he thought, and he was
so happy that he gave the shark one
last chance.

"But this really is it," he said. "Any
more swallowing and you're off."

"Don't worry, I'll be good now," said
Noah's shark. "You'll see."

Noah's shark was good for three days.
For three whole days, she
worked hard and did

as she was told. For three whole nights, she kept her mouth to herself and swallowed only air. But air cannot satisfy a hungry shark's appetite. Air cannot stop the rumbling of a hungry shark's stomach. One night, Noah's shark could stand it no longer.

She was so hungry, she tried to swallow the first animal she came across. It was Mr Giraffe. Now giraffes are much more difficult to swallow than rabbits or dodos – especially when they wake up when you're only halfway through swallowing them.

Mr Giraffe snorted angrily and tried to pull his head out of the shark's

mouth. But Noah's shark held on tight. Mr Giraffe pulled one way; Noah's shark pulled the other and so it went on, until Noah arrived.

Boy, was he cross!

"Let go at once!" he shouted, and Noah's shark did. Mr Giraffe shook his head and it bumped against the ceiling.

"Oh my," he gasped. His neck was now almost as long as his body! (If you have ever wondered why giraffes' necks are so long – there's your answer.)

Noah glared at his shark. He was shaking with anger.

"Get off my boat! Now!" he shouted.

This time, Noah's shark knew she'd blown it. She'd gone too far. Sadly, she slithered away and, with a last wistful glance behind, she jumped into the sea.

Now Noah's shark didn't think she'd like the water. She thought it would be cold and nasty and no fun at all. But she was wrong. The moment she dropped down into the salty sea and the water closed over her, she felt oddly at home, as if this was where she should have been all along. She could move much faster in the water than she ever could on land. Flicking her tail she shot through the sea, her sharp fin cutting the water like a knife through cream. Yes, this was the life for her!

She was sorry that she'd let Noah down, but she wasn't sorry to have left the boat. A boat wasn't the place for a shark, she decided. She was much better off down here in the ocean. And there was so much food! All she had to do

was swim along with her mouth open
and hundreds of fish swam in. Now that
was something really worth swallowing!

Chapter Five

At last, after forty days and nights at sea, Noah's boat came in sight of land. Noah sent two of his best birds, Mr and Mrs Raven, to have a look and see what the land was like.

Unfortunately, a sudden gust of wind blew them off course and they ended up

at the Tower of London. So Noah sent
Mr and Mrs Dove. They came back
with a big bunch of lovely ripe bananas,
so Noah knew that he had found the
place he was searching for.

Later that day, Noah's boat came to land. The animals disembarked two by two, followed by Noah and his family. What a party they had!

Now Noah's shark heard the noise of the party and she swam up close to the land.

"Noah!" she called. "Noah! Come and talk to me!"

Noah was a little bit wary, but he recognised the voice of his shark and he went down to the water's edge to see her. The truth was that he was actually kind of fond of that shark, despite what she'd done. He was rather pleased to hear her voice again. He knew, though, that he couldn't have her back again in his world.

"How are you, Mrs Shark?" he said.

"Is the sea treating you OK?"

"It's great," said Mrs Shark. "Why don't you come on in. The water's lovely."

Old Noah shook his head and smiled. He was no fool.

"No, thanks," he said. "I don't fancy getting swallowed up. You stick to the water and I'll stay on dry land. Then we'll both be happy. Is that a deal?"

"It's a deal," said Mrs Shark.

And so it has stayed to this day. Well, actually, now and then people do go wandering around in the shark's world and get themselves swallowed up. But you can't blame the sharks. They can't help swallowing. And besides, you don't see sharks wandering around on the land, do you?

If you enjoyed this story, why not read another *Skylarks* book?

Josie's Garden
by David Orme and Martin Remphry

Josie lives in a high-rise flat in town with her mum and brother. More than anything else in the world, Josie wants a garden. When Josie and her friend, Meena, discover an abandoned and over-grown garden near their school, Josie is delighted and decides to make the garden her own. But sometimes, things are not quite as simple as they first seem…

Merbaby

by Penny Kendal and Claudia Venturini

One day at the beach, Anna, Ellie and Joe find a funny-looking fish in a rock pool. To their surprise, they find that the fish is a baby mermaid! They take the merbaby home in a bucket and keep it a secret from Mum. But, four-year-old Joe isn't very good at keeping secrets, and soon the merbaby is in danger. Will Anna and Ellie be able to save her?

Carving the Sea Path

by Kathryn White and Evelyn Duverne

When Samuel first moves to the Arctic, he is rude and unfriendly. But Irniq gives him a chance, and the boys become friends. Then, as the summer comes to an end, the boys quarrel and drift apart. One day, Irniq finds a trapped whale under the ice, and doesn't know what to do. Luckily, Samuel appears and knows exactly who can help. Will the boys save the whale in time?

The Emperor's New Clothes
by Louise John and Serena Curmi

There once lived an emperor who was proud and vain and spent all his money on clothes. One day, two scoundrels arrived at the palace and persuaded the emperor that they could weave magical cloth. He set them to work making him a fine set of robes.

But the emperor had a lesson to learn, and his new clothes were quite a sight to behold!

Skylarks titles include:

Awkward Annie
by Julia Williams and Tim Archbold
HB 9780237533847 / PB 9780237534028

Sleeping Beauty
by Louise John and Natascia Ugliano
HB 9780237533861 / PB 9780237534042

Detective Derek
by Karen Wallace and Beccy Blake
HB 9780237533885 / PB 9780237534066

Hurricane Season
by David Orme and Doreen Lang
HB 9780237533892 / PB 9780237534073

Spiggy Red
by Penny Dolan and Cinzia Battistel
HB 9780237533854 / PB 9780237534035

London's Burning
by Pauline Francis and Alessandro Baldanzi
HB 9780237533878 / PB 9780237534059

The Black Knight
by Mick Gowar and Graham Howells
HB 9780237535803 / PB 9780237535926

Ghost Mouse
by Karen Wallace and Beccy Blake
HB 9780237535827 / PB 9780237535940

Yasmin's Parcels
by Jill Atkins and Lauren Tobia
HB 9780237535858 / PB 9780237535971

Muffin
by Anne Rooney and Sean Julian
HB 9780237535810 / PB 9780237535933

Tallulah and the Tea Leaves
by Louise John and Vian Oelofsen
HB 9780237535841 / PB 9780237535964

The Big Purple Wonderbook
by Enid Richemont and Helen Jackson
HB 9780237535834 / PB 9780237535957

Noah's Shark
by Alan Durant and Holly Surplice
HB 9780237539047 / PB 9780237538910

The Emperor's New Clothes
by Louise John and Serena Curmi
HB 9780237539085 / PB 9780237538958

Carving the Sea Path
by Kathryn White and Evelyn Duverne
HB 9780237539030 / PB 9780237538903

Merbaby
by Penny Kendal and Claudia Venturini
HB 9780237539078 / PB 9780237538941

The Lion and the Gypsy
by Jillian Powell and Heather Deen
HB 9780237539054 / PB 9780237538927

Josie's Garden
by David Orme and Martin Remphry
HB 9780237539061 / PB 9780237538934